GREAT ESCAPES

JOURNEY TO FREEDOM, 1838

GREAT ESCAPES

JOURNEY TO FREEDOM, 1838

BY SHERRI WINSTON

EDITED BY MICHAEL TEITELBAUM

HARPER

An Imprint of HarperCollins*Publishers*

To my late uncle MacArthur Winston,
whose imagination and fiery spirit
were hallmarks of my childhood. —S.W.

Great Escapes #2: Journey to Freedom, 1838

Photo credit: page 85: U.S. National Archives
and Records Administration
 For information address HarperCollins Children's Books, a division of HarperCollins Publishers, 195 Broadway, New York, NY 10007.
www.harpercollinschildrens.com

Library of Congress Cataloging-in-Publication Data
Names: Winston, Sherri, author. | Teitelbaum, Michael, editor.
Title: Journey to freedom, 1838 / Sherri Winston ; edited by Michael Teitelbaum.
Description: First edition. | New York : HarperCollins, [2020] | Series: Great escapes ; #2 | Includes bibliographical references. | Summary: In this retelling of an episode from Uncle Tom's Cabin, the slave Eliza Harris resolves to escape with her two-year-old son across the frozen Ohio River to prevent her master from selling the boy. Includes historical notes on Harriet Beecher Stowe, slavery in America, the Fugitive slave laws, and the Underground Railroad.
Identifiers: LCCN 2019026613 | ISBN 978-0-06-286039-2 (hardcover) | ISBN 978-0-06-286038-5 (paperback)
Subjects: LCSH: Slaves—United States—Juvenile fiction. | Fugitive slaves—Juvenile fiction. | African American women—19th century—Juvenile fiction. | Plantation life—Kentucky—Juvenile fiction. | Slavery—United States—Juvenile fiction. | Kentucky—History—19th century—Juvenile fiction. | CYAC: Fugitive slaves—Fiction. | African Americans—Fiction. | Plantation life—Kentucky—Fiction. | Slavery—Fiction. | Kentucky—History—19th century—Fiction.
Classification: LCC PZ7.W7536 Jo 2020 | DDC 813.6 [Fic]—dc23
LC record available at https://lccn.loc.gov/2019026613

Typography by David Curtis
20 21 22 23 24 PC/LSCH 10 9 8 7 6 5 4 3 2 1
❖
First Edition

INTRODUCTION

Readers, educators, historians, and even students may wonder why a modern-day African American author would use the novel of a nineteenth century white woman abolitionist as the base for her own writing.

The answer is simple:

Without Harriet Beecher Stowe immortalizing the plight, fire, gumption, and determination of a black slave woman willing to risk her life to save her young child, there would be no story to tell.

Stowe took information she gathered about the real woman's daring escape to freedom, shaped and molded it as authors do, and created the character of Eliza Harris. Subsequently, Eliza Harris became one of the most celebrated and recognized figures in American history, despite being an amalgam of Stowe's research. The writings of other abolitionists of the day, such as John Rankin, John Rankin Jr., and Levi Coffin, back up Stowe's account of Eliza's river crossing, although since the details in their stories differ, it's possible—even likely—that they refer to more than one woman.

In fact, many such women, men, and children escaped slavery by crossing the Ohio. Since the real Eliza, like most slaves, was not able to read and write, she did not leave behind any writings of her own as far as we know. We know of her story and others like it only through the writings of abolitionists, like Stowe, Rankin, and others. It is impossible to know for certain the details of her life. Thus, I have done my best to portray her escape as closely as possible to the way it was originally told by Stowe and Rankin.

Stowe, through imagination and research for her novel *Uncle Tom's Cabin*, gave us a first look at what Eliza's life was like before that fateful crossing. A look at what could drive a woman to such desperation, her small child in tow.

Keep in mind that before Stowe was a novelist, she was a journalist. She did not set out to write a best-selling novel. Her intent was to create a few articles for the abolitionist press—articles that would illuminate the hardships of slavery, using composite characters based on her research. Her goal was to rail against the Fugitive Slave Act of 1850, which compelled free states to assist in the capture of runaway slaves.

The National Era in Washington, DC, published the first part of what would later become Stowe's seminal novel on the topic of slavery on June 5, 1851. In the spirit of her novel, her articles, and her research, and in the tradition of the many retellings of the story from the nineteenth century, I have retold Stowe's tale, while also adding fictional elements that are my own. For example, in my story, the Seldons are based on Stowe's composite family the Shelbys. I also took from the accounts of John Rankin and his son,

John Rankin Jr., with regard to the later events of Eliza's journey. Canadian newspaper articles from the 1930s suggest Eliza's grave rests in Dresden, Ontario, Canada, near the grave of Josiah Henson, believed to have been the inspiration for the character of Uncle Tom. Whether these claims are true or fiction is lost to history.

I chose to retell the story of Eliza Harris loosely following its original source from *Uncle Tom's Cabin,* in homage to Stowe, while also adding details of my own as a way to bring back to life a figure who for too long has been forgotten. Without Stowe, the figure known as Eliza Harris and thousands like her likely would have remained unknown. I hope you enjoy my reimagining of the real Eliza as she might have been. For more about my sources, check out the bibliography at the back of this book.

Sherri Winston

Chapter One

A HARSH REALITY

Eliza Harris pressed her body against the house.

Winter air chilled her skin. The conversation she overheard chilled her soul.

"He is willing to pay top dollar," said the voice belonging to Ainsley Seldon. "That little boy, Harry, plus a few others, gonna bring in the money I need."

Eliza felt as if an icicle was being shoved directly into her heart.

Mr. Seldon was selling a baby. A boy.

Her son!

Eliza was a slave. Mr. Seldon was her master, which meant he owned Eliza, her husband, and their son, the same as if they were horses or shoes. Slaves were not treated like human beings. As a young enslaved woman, Eliza was forced to live apart from her husband because that was how Mr. Seldon wanted it.

She had already buried two children—both died of pneumonia. The idea of losing another son because of the evil practice of slavery was more than she could bear.

Rage bubbled inside her.

She clenched her hands into fists.

Glancing upward, Eliza saw the evening sun painting the Kentucky sky a deep fire orange. Fat clouds laced with shades of charcoal gray approached as night began to fall. The scent of pine trees and winter snow filled her nostrils. Her breath came out in hard gusts.

In the distance, a wolf howled, hungry and prowling for its dinner. *Even he is free*, Eliza thought bitterly.

She attempted to move closer to the front porch where the men stood with their cigars—everyone knew that Mrs. Seldon didn't like the smell of smoke in the house. As Eliza stepped, a twig cracked under her foot.

The sound echoed like a gunshot in the night.

"Who's there?" said Mr. Morgan, Mr. Seldon's guest. Then footsteps, heavy feet on frozen snow. The men.

They were coming!

Eliza knew that if they caught her, she might get whipped to death before she could save her baby from the auction block. A slave found eavesdropping could expect punishment. She was in grave danger.

Looking around, she followed the trail back to the kitchen door. She heard the men's boots scrabbling over slick ice.

If she slipped on the icy puddles that coated the path, Eliza might fall and break her neck. Or worse. She could be discovered where she didn't belong.

The footsteps grew closer. Louder. If she could just make it to the edge of the house . . .

"Anybody back there? Ya better come on out!" called Mr. Morgan. He was a rough man with a

coarse manner. Eliza did not welcome the way he looked at her when he came to call on Mr. Seldon.

She dared not look back now.

With her heart pounding and muscles tight, Eliza made it to the corner. She threw herself against the back of the house.

Her body was shaking.

Not because she was tired. Not because she was cold.

But because she was angry.

She thought of her baby. Little Harry.

His faced popped into her mind and the image made her gasp. She wanted to hold him, kiss him, and stroke his hair.

Eliza and Mrs. Seldon had a regular nightly routine—Eliza would help get the Seldon children ready for bed as well as help their mother undo waist cinchers or difficult back hooks on her dresses.

Now all Eliza wanted to do was see her son. Instead, she heard her name being called. Mrs. Seldon's face appeared at the door.

"For heaven's sake, Eliza. You look like you've

seen a ghost. Before you go home, could you come inside again? Won't take but a minute. I need your help."

Eliza felt the rush of her own blood pounding in her ears. When she blew out a breath, great plumes of frosty air hovered before her face. There was always one more this or one more that. Always one more thing to keep her from her son.

Eliza tried to marshal her expression and extinguish the fire in her eyes. "Yes, ma'am," she said. Inside or outside, she needed to get away from Mr. Seldon and his rough visitor. She followed the lady of the house, helped the woman with one last task, then hurried away from the Seldons as quickly as she could.

Eliza moved swiftly but carefully across the icy ground. She was a young woman with golden-brown skin and thick, curly hair worn braided into a thick crown. She had never been extra girly. Instead, Eliza loved the outdoors. Loved the smell of fresh air and the sight of birds flying free in the sky.

And she loved the feeling of moving her body.

She had been a good runner when she was a young girl—just as good as any boy.

It didn't take long for Eliza to reach the small hill that led down to where she and the rest of Mr. Seldon's two dozen or so slaves lived. Within minutes she was at the door of Miss Sadie's cabin.

"How do, Eliza?" said the old woman who often looked after Harry. She sat in a rocking chair. A small fire burned in the hearth behind her. Wrinkles like lines on an antique map were etched into her dark skin.

She frowned. "Liza? What's wrong, child?" the woman asked.

Eliza entered the house and stopped, standing in the doorway, staring down at her baby. Harry was almost two. He had fat cheeks and wide, dark eyes. His tiny hands reached toward the ceiling of the old shack.

Again the older woman asked, "Liza? You come on in here and sit. You letting out all my warmth. What's got into you? Look like you done seen a fright."

After a moment more, Eliza collapsed to her

knees in front of Miss Sadie's rocker. She scooped Little Harry into her arms and held him tight. The baby fussed and giggled. His woolly head of glorious kinky hair tickled her face.

Her heart burned with love and pride.

Finally, when she had absorbed every bit of him that she could, she pulled away enough to look at the older woman. Miss Sadie continued to stare at her with concern.

"He wants to sell my baby!" she cried.

"Who?" asked Miss Sadie.

"Mr. Seldon. He was talking to Mr. Morgan after dinner, smoking their cigars on the porch like usual. I overheard him. He wants to sell Harry."

Miss Sadie gave a quick nod of understanding. Then slowly she shook her head. She had been a slave since she was a girl. She had witnessed so many families torn apart—one person sold to one family, while the wife, brother, sister, or child was sold to another—that she had simply lost count.

"It's our burden to bear, child. I'm so sorry," she said.

Eliza's eyes burned with fire to match the flames in the hearth.

"I will never let that happen!" she said. "Ain't nobody selling my baby!"

Miss Sadie was shocked by the young woman's words and look of determination. "Try to keep yourself calm, Liza. Won't do you no good getting in trouble for something you cannot control."

Eliza, however, was not about to calm down. She thanked Sadie, as usual, for keeping an eye on Harry. Then she took Harry and went to the cabin she shared with Miss Mattie, another old slave woman. Miss Mattie was such a good cook that the Seldons hired her out sometimes.

A surprise awaited Eliza inside—her husband.

"George!" she said.

Balancing Baby Harry, swaddled in a bundle of cloths, Eliza rushed toward him.

"It's the middle of the week. You don't normally come 'round till Sunday," she said, giving him a tight hug.

He held her, then stepped back and took the baby out of her arms.

George Harris cuddled his son, then stared long and hard at his faithful wife. Eliza sensed something was not right.

He edged her toward the far side of the tiny cabin. Miss Mattie said her how-dos and left, sensing the couple needed privacy.

Once they were alone, George let out a deep breath and bent to one knee so he could look into his wife's eyes. Eliza sat on a rickety wooden chair near the hearth. He placed their son in her arms.

"What?" she said.

"I'm leaving tonight," he said. "They sending me and Amos on an errand. Only this time, we ain't coming back. We just gonna keep on walking. It'll take 'em at least a week to realize."

"No!" she said, shooting to her feet. Her husband straightened.

"Let me finish, Eliza," he pleaded. "I know it'll be hard. But I've met some people. Good people nearby. People with connections to freedom. They gonna help us get to Canada. And after I get situated, I'll come back for you."

Eliza Harris, like every other slave in these parts, had heard many tales about the escape routes that came to be known as the Underground Railroad. It wasn't a steam locomotive that traveled below the earth. Instead, it referred to hundreds of people—black and white—who provided shelter and guidance to those who wanted to escape slavery or already had.

WHAT WAS THE UNDERGROUND RAILROAD?

All aboard! Next stop, freedom! The Underground Railroad, a system of shelters and routes designed to help escaped slaves travel north, began in the late 1700s and continued through the Civil War. Although the source of the name is unknown, it is believed to have originated in the 1830s when American railroads were booming. Rather than being made of iron and propelled by coal, the Underground Railroad used human ingenuity, black people's knowledge of the landscape, and a variety of transportation modes. Free African Americans and whites worked together as "conductors," people who hosted and led escaped slaves on their journeys to the northern United States as well as Canada.

"George," Eliza said, "Mr. Seldon's gonna sell Harry! Our baby! I won't let him, George. I won't."

For a long time, George held his wife. He tried to console her, tried to assure her that it would be easier for him to find his way to the Underground Railroad alone and then return for her and Harry after he was sure they had a place to live free.

Even so, after he was gone, Eliza lay awake that night staring at the ceiling. She felt the warmth of her child pressed against her. In the dim light from the dying coals on the hearth, she made out rough shapes of scrap furnishings. Leftovers and hand-me-downs.

A terrible cold draft seeped between the wooden boards around her. With each harsh gust of wind, the small building seemed to sway.

Human beings ought not to live like this, she thought. Mr. Seldon took better care of his horses than he did his slaves. She pictured her husband disappearing into the night. The light of freedom leading the way like the North Star.

Her heart thudded in her chest. She feared it was loud enough to wake Harry. It was beating with the strength and courage of her ancestors. She'd lost her mother to slavery, having been separated from her years ago. She'd been a baby when her father was taken.

She squeezed Harry against her side.

"I won't let nobody take you, Harry," she whispered against his cheek. He cooed and turned over, nuzzling into her bosom. His softness and sweetness were enough to make her want to cry.

Eliza knew, however, that she had no time for tears.

It was time for action.

She would protect her baby.

Or by God, she'd die trying.

Chapter Two

THE FINAL STRAW

The next morning Eliza felt a knot growing in her belly. A flood of emotions gripped her—fear, anger, sadness, rage! As she dressed Baby Harry her hands shook.

She floated through her workday in a daze.

The morning routine inside the Seldons' house was rigorous as usual. Eliza worked steadily, emptying chamber pots, getting water from the well, and helping the missus, as well as the children, dress. Eliza did her best to keep her focus. At times when her mind went back to what she'd overheard the day before, her hands shook and her knees threatened to buckle.

Later, while she was darning socks in front of the hearth and the missus was embroidering, Mrs. Seldon stared hard at her and asked, "Eliza, what is deviling your soul?"

"Ma'am?" Eliza said.

"Oh, Eliza!" harrumphed Mrs. Seldon. "You cannot hide anything from me. I know you well enough to notice when you are not yourself. Tell me, what is troubling you? Perhaps I can help."

Eliza took a long moment to consider. Now she let her gaze stray to the window, avoiding eye contact with Mrs. Seldon. Outside, the Seldon children made whooping sounds of delight that filtered through the frosty windows. The children sounded so free.

Unlike poor Baby Harry, who was not free at all.

Eliza drew a big breath and exhaled.

"Missus," she began. "I—I heard something yesterday that I oughtn't have."

Mrs. Seldon dropped her hands to her lap and sat straighter in the chair. She said, "Go on."

Eliza swallowed, then plunged ahead.

"I overheard Mr. Seldon. He was talking to his friend 'bout Harry," Eliza said.

Mrs. Seldon frowned. "About who?" she asked.

Eliza didn't bother to hide the heat that flashed behind her eyes like lightning over ice.

"My boy, Mrs. Seldon. My baby."

The white woman set the embroidery gently in her lap. Her cheeks reddened. Such outbursts or shows of emotion from Eliza were unheard of. Eliza suddenly didn't care what the woman of Seldon House thought of her manners.

"All right, Eliza," Mrs. Seldon said, one eyebrow lifted, no doubt taken aback by the abruptness of Eliza's tone. "Why was Mr. Seldon talking about your boy? Is the child sick? Has he done something—"

"No ma'am!" Eliza said, cutting her off. "He ain't done nothing. He's just a baby. But I heard your husband telling the other man that he was going to sell Harry. Sell him right away from me!"

Mrs. Seldon gasped. She stood so quickly that the fabric she'd been embroidering fell onto the floor.

"Eliza!" she said. "You mustn't say such things. Ainsley would never do that."

Despair and agitation squeezed at Eliza's heart

and lungs. She sprang up just as quickly, her fists clenched at her sides. Her mind was nearly insane with grief.

"He said it. He did, missus. He said he needed the money, and some other man said he'd pay good for a young one like Harry. I was coming from the barn and they was on the porch. I heard 'em clear as day!" Eliza sagged, breathless with the effort of retelling the story.

"I will talk with Ainsley when he returns this evening," Mrs. Seldon said. Taking hold of Eliza's arm and giving it a firm squeeze, she continued, "Surely Ainsley would not do such a thing. You will see."

Even as she listened to the words spilling with such confidence from Mrs. Seldon's prim lips, Eliza was forming a plan.

A plan that had no place for waiting to see what someone else would do.

It was time, Eliza knew, for her to decide for herself—*do* for herself! She wasn't waiting for George to come back for her and Harry. They were going to find him!

◆◆◆

Eliza got confirmation that she could rely on no one but herself later that evening. Mr. and Mrs. Seldon were in their upstairs bedroom. Eliza had been working in the kitchen when the youngest of the Seldon children thumped down the back stairs, rubbing his eyes and calling to her.

"Miss Liza, why is your baby going away?" the child asked.

At first, Eliza frowned. The golden-haired youngster was clearly sleepy.

"Child, it's your bedtime," she said, smiling. Then realization set in as she understood what the boy had said.

"But Miss Liza, I heard Papa say Harry got to go away, and then Mama, she cried. Is you gonna let 'em do it? Take Harry away? I like to play with Harry." The boy had played with her son all through the summer, the two of them laughing and shrieking and running.

Like equals. For this boy such a thing was natural. For her son, she knew the idea of being equal would be as unnatural as talking to the moon and having it talk back.

With a very hoarse whisper, she told the child to go on up to his room and his mama would come around and say good night.

"Go on, child. Go on to bed. Let me worry about Harry," she said.

Every sound in the house felt magnified. The snap-crackle of embers in the fireplace; the cold chill of gusting night breezes against frozen windowpanes; the pitty-pat tapping of horse hooves on straw and frozen ground in the barns. Sound carried on the cold night air. The house settled in. All was calm.

Except for Eliza. She wasn't calm. Not at all.

Chapter Three

FREEDOM CRIES

The night crept by in aching seconds.

Tick. Tick. Tick, went the branches clacking in the wind.

Snores floated softly from old Miss Mattie who shared Eliza's broken-down shack. Their rickety sleeping cots formed an L shape in the dark. Baby Harry lay beside Eliza cooing in his sleep, peaceful as the snowflakes falling quietly from the night sky.

Eliza felt each minute pass. She tossed and turned, her insides knotted with worry. When she rolled onto her side, thin wisps of moonlight glinting off the frozen ice and snow outside illuminated her sleeping baby.

He was free when he slept—free to dream. What kind of dreams did he dare have if she let him grow up a slave? A slave with no mama to love him.

The thought of that made her want to cry out. Pain pierced her insides as surely as if she'd been stuck with a kitchen knife. Escape was her only choice. Yet she knew from stories told by other slaves that few women managed to get free. It wasn't uncommon for women—and men—to return after being gone for several days because they had no other place to go.

To quiet her mind, Eliza concentrated on the lyrics of old spiritual songs—songs whose lyrics spoke of gourds in the sky and the brightest stars; songs meant to help escaping slaves navigate their passage to freedom.

Eliza thought back to long-tucked-away memories of lyrics. Her pounding heart slowly found comfort in the words. Gradually, she felt her pulse slow and grow calmer. She knew in her gut how this was to be done. She'd heard it all before. In songs and in hushed conversations among her elders. Words whispered between her and George on pillows when they'd dared live as man and wife. How was George doing? Where was he at this exact moment? Was he safe? Would she ever be able to find him again?

She remembered other slaves murmuring about escape. How it was better to attempt freedom in winter because the Ohio River, an obstacle for Kentucky slaves and others in the South, was frozen in winter and therefore easier to cross. Most slaves didn't learn to swim. Crossing when the river was running wasn't much of an option. Being that the Ohio River was less than a half mile across, it was walkable—so long as it remained solid.

Eliza knew from the old songs that finding the North Star and following it in the right direction could mean the difference between freedom and heartbreak for her and Harry, same as it had for so many others escaping north.

Finally, Eliza succumbed to the night, falling into a fitful slumber. However, when the time came to wake and prepare for the day, she was not tired. She was not hesitant.

She was ready.

The next day her plan came together.

Hours crept along, Eliza feeling her anticipation build. And build. And . . . build.

A feeling so intense it was like hunger.

Freedom. Her heart raced with the feeling of never needing or wanting anything so badly before in her life.

Why had she not done this sooner? she wondered.

The idea of freedom, of not having to fear she'd have her baby taken from her, created a fire in her belly. Freedom to live with the man she loved; freedom to learn to read and have the right to educate her son. Freedom to be human.

Eliza worked hard all that day. Watery afternoon daylight leaked into the children's bedroom windows. Eliza was putting away their freshly washed and ironed linens. Fine bedsheets. Much nicer than she or Harry dared imagine. She stole a quick glance over her shoulder. Then, certain she was alone, Eliza took one of the freshly laundered and pressed sheets and shoved it under her blouse. It would come in handy later.

When dinner had been served and cleared, Eliza dutifully donned her shawl. She loaded up the bin to take the leftovers out to feed the livestock. Leftover chicken was usually set aside for Mr. Seldon, who had a habit of eating during the night. She managed to get a chicken thigh inside her hand just as Mrs. Seldon entered the kitchen.

"I'm going out to the pen, ma'am," Eliza said.

"Very well," the woman answered, barely sparing her a look. Eliza had noticed that the missus had made no mention of her talk with Mr. Seldon, no word on his choice. Eliza knew that was because what she had overheard was right.

Once out of sight, rather than empty the scraps in the animals' pen, Eliza took bits of bread and found a small gourd she could fill with water. That done, she washed her hands in the snow and secured her looted foodstuffs in the folds of her clothes.

Eliza didn't want to dally. She was afraid she might start raining chunks of stolen food or bedclothes. Back inside, Eliza said her good evenings, and was ready to dash away. Yet she allowed herself one last look at the woman—Mrs. Seldon, with her cornsilk-yellow hair, thin face, and pale-blue eyes. Eliza also took in the kitchen of which she knew every inch because she'd scrubbed and polished it on her hands and knees; she caught a glimpse of the two younger Seldon children rushing toward the stairs. She'd attended both their births, caught the babies right in her hands on account of the doctor being tipsy.

So much history.

If she were lucky, she would never see them again!

It didn't take long after gathering Harry into her arms and heading to her quarters for Eliza to fall into a deep, dreamless sleep. So much adrenaline had pumped through her body all that day. Now she needed rest.

When she awoke in the dark, an owl hooted into the night. She rose quickly, going to the one small window in the shack and pressing her cheek against the cold pane.

Then she turned and moved noiselessly around the cramped space. She collected the few items she had managed to grab from the main house. If she were caught, stolen food would be the least of her worries.

The moon sat high and bright, glittering like a debutante's smile. She had at least seven hours before sunrise to reach the river.

It was time.

She wrapped her sleepy child in whatever cloth she could find. She did the same for herself. The gentle snores of Miss Mattie felt like a lullaby. Eliza wondered if she should wake the old woman and say goodbye.

In the end, she decided against it.

Eliza used the same ingenuity that allowed enslaved women to tie their babies against them while they picked cotton or tended fields. Harry barely squirmed as she took a bedsheet she'd slipped out of the Seldon home and fixed it into a sling. Harry's body pressed into her own, and their hearts played two tempos of the same song.

A deep breath, then she held her boy close

against her chest and pushed out into the night air.

A few moments later, she stopped just beyond the threshold.

There was still time to go back.

Eliza looked down at the face of her child. Harry wrinkled his nose, smelling the fresh, sweet scent of pine trees and frozen earth. Eliza almost released a bitter laugh at the thought of the overseer and her master, Mr. Seldon, thrashing about in the cold in search of her when they realized what she'd done.

The boy nuzzled closer to her warmth and settled down.

Turning to give one last look at the shack she'd called home for so many years, she swung around and walked carefully toward the stand of pines leading into the frozen woods.

The moon's white face stared down at her.

It was time to make her escape!

Eliza moved as quickly as she could across the frozen ground, breathing heavily into the frosty night, her breath fogging the air ahead of her. The Seldons' plantation home and farm was set several miles south and west of the Ohio River. Eliza had learned that from listening to talk around campfires with other slaves.

She made herself inhale and exhale slowly for several seconds, stilling her nerves.

You know how to do this, Eliza! she told herself.

She got her bearings, and figured out by looking into the sky and at the lean of the trees where to head first. She set off, slowly at first, then gaining speed.

For several minutes, she raced as though set free from a cage. The cold air sliced the back of her throat. The ice and brush of the woods threatened to steal her footing. Still, she ran. She ran because for the first time in her life, she felt free to run. Free to go faster and faster. She felt . . . free.

When the freezing air began to turn her teeth into icicles and glue her tongue to her lips, she slowed. Eliza was out of breath, panting. Harry squirmed. She'd taken a towel and made a pillow for him that was wedged between his cheek and her layers of knit shawls and woolens. It kept him from banging against her as she ran. Now she sank back against a bare oak tree for support.

Above, the sky was dark and clear. Eliza forced herself to control her breathing. She had to get oriented again, make sure she was continuing in the right direction. Make sure she could conserve her energy to last throughout the night.

Eliza remembered how when she was a young girl, she would sit and listen to her elders discuss news from up North. And now she was going there herself! The tales sometimes frightened her; other times they filled her with excitement. A sense of adventure. And hope. One night, she remembered, an old man from the slave quarters taught her a valuable skill. It was after dark. Firelight flickered, keeping away the bugs, and a few folks sang spirituals or songs of freedom. The old man pointed heavenward and said:

"That's the Big Dipper and the Little Dipper."

He went on to teach her how to line up the stars to find her way. He urged her to watch the sky and taught her to spot Orion, which was brightest in winter. Orion's belt pointed northwest. If she followed his arm, she would be heading toward the river.

How her heart had thudded in her chest. Talking

to the old man had felt like going to school. Eliza had never had a chance to go to school. She could think of no greater gift for Harry.

Eliza recalled that years-ago conversation as she clutched her baby to her body. She stared into the sky for several minutes, until she was certain she was seeing the same collection of stars the old man had long ago pointed out. Once she knew for sure she had located Orion and the North Star she drew another breath and started on her route.

She knew the Ohio River was several hours away by foot. But that was walking, not running. If she kept her wits about her, and kept an eye out for wild animals, she'd have plenty of time to arrive at the river and cross before the ice began to melt and become slick beneath the daylight sun.

At least, she hoped she would.

She moved steadily on through the trees, wondering where George might be at this moment. As she walked, the stars slid silently across the sky. Wind pushed at naked limbs high overhead. Slithery noises crawled along in the darkness. Not birds. Something bigger? Eliza became more aware of her surroundings. She'd never been so far away from the plantation. Just as she'd heard stories of brave escapes by desperate heroic slaves, she'd also heard of grisly ends that came thanks to wolves, coyotes, or other nocturnal beasts.

Something skittered in her chest, and her arms instinctively drew protectively around her son. Icy snow crunched beneath her feet, but she knew she had to keep moving.

Finally, after hours of walking, she stopped in a copse of woods to rest. Beneath the folds of her layers of clothes and rags, she'd hidden the tiny gourd she'd filled with water. Despite the cold, sweat tickled the back of her neck, curling her hair around the edges.

Eliza found a stump and dropped onto it. She sipped slowly from the gourd, feeling the cool water touch her throat and soothe her parched mouth. While seated, she readjusted the blankets around Baby Harry. His eyes popped open.

The boy sniffed and found the cold unagreeable. He let out a loud yelp.

"Shh . . . shh . . . shh," urged Eliza. Then the boy cooed and wiggled on her lap. Eliza was watching him, seeing the curtain of sleep tug at his eyelids, when she heard another noise.

This time, the sound was low and thick, like thunder growling under a mountain.

What was that?

She craned her neck to get a better look.

Nothing.

Then it came again. Definitely not nothing.

It was . . . a growl!

Fear sliced at her heart. She peered into the thick blanket of night that lay above the snow-covered earth searching for an animal that could cause that sound.

Out of the night, a glowing pair of eyes stared back.

Chapter Four

DANGER IN THE DARK

Was it a wolf? A coyote?

It was winter and food was scarce for animals. The beast, whatever it was, was no doubt hungry.

Looking around her, Eliza grabbed a huge stick that had been leaning against the stump where she'd sat. She stepped onto the stump and raised the heavy stick overhead with one hand.

"Aaaaaargh!" she snarled back at the woods. She shook with rage and fear. After fleeing her master to save her son, she was not about to let an animal tear him from her. Not without a fight!

The mix of emotions left her feeling wild. How dare this creature—whatever it was—threaten her and her son? And how dare it stand between her and freedom?

Eliza puffed up her body and made herself as big and threatening as possible. Someone at the slave quarters had once told her if she ever encountered a wild animal while out gathering water or wood for the house, she should not act afraid and she should try to make herself appear large and scary.

Rough, craggy edges from the stick bit into her hand. She realized she was squeezing it so hard her fingers were going numb. Eliza bit back a cry of frustration. She needed to make noise, make the beast fear her. Yet making too much noise might alarm her sleeping son and create a whole new peril, reaching the ears of humans in the dark.

Steeling her nerve, Eliza gathered her courage. More growling and rustling from the darkness made her skin crawl. Clutching her son tight against her, she gave a nearby tree a hard thwack. The baby, always a sound sleeper, continued to breathe rhythmically.

THWACK!

She banged the stick again against a tree, hoping, praying, that she'd traveled far enough into the thicket that the commotion would go unnoticed by people on nearby farms. Or her son.

In the dark, Eliza knew she was an inky blot to the animal. In her mind's eye she pictured what she must have looked like—swirling shapes, teeth bared, wild-eyed, and holding a strange bundle.

When Eliza finally stopped long enough to take a deep breath, she realized the woods were once again quiet. Listening hard, she heard no other wild noises filtering from beyond the bushes.

Had the creature left?

Eliza felt her ankles turn to mush. She sagged with relief. Harry began to wail, and it took several minutes to quiet him. All the while, every hoot, sniffle, or snuffle that came from the trees felt like the fiery end of a branding iron sending shocks throughout her body.

Her breath caught in her chest. She let her gaze travel along the footprints in the snow, marking the path that the unseen animal had taken. Thank goodness it was in the opposite direction of where she was headed. That was all she could hope for, at least for now.

Eliza filled her lungs with air cold enough to freeze the moon, then blew out a plume of steam. She was scared. But she was determined, too. Going back was not an option. Not even if she encountered a hundred wild beasts.

Have mercy! she thought, hoping that she would not find even a single additional nocturnal creature.

She grasped the stick in one hand and her son with the other and continued her trek.

For hours she trudged through thorny briars and underbrush, fallen twigs and forest debris. Every so often a small animal would scurry past or move in the trees above. Eliza steeled her nerves. She had to keep going.

Snow and ice had given way to the forest floor. Eliza believed she could smell the water, frozen or not. She pushed herself harder. Every so often, she'd feel lost beneath the thick canopy of gnarled branches, but she forced herself to continue her journey.

Exhaustion tugged at her body and made her limbs leaden. Baby Harry's eyes were wide. He seemed to sense the anxiety of his mama. His dark eyes clouded, and he began to whimper.

Eliza didn't stop to shush him. She was focused on moving forward. The trees were thinning. The wind felt stronger. Soon she realized that overhead cover had disappeared. Once again she stood beneath the winter sky. The stars were melting away. The purple sheen of daylight began to form a thin ribbon to the east.

Morning loomed near.

She had to be close.

Urgency swept through her limbs and she practically staggered. She was running so hard, blood pumped in her ears with a roar. Something was rustling the brush ahead of her, but she paid it no attention. She kept running and felt a stiff wind sting her face. She broke through the bushes and saw it stretching out before her.

The Ohio River!

It lay flat and still and dusted in snow beneath the fading moonlight.

Baby Harry let out a long, loud cry. Eliza wanted to let out a yell as well. The river was coated in ice. The quarter-mile expanse made it easy for Eliza to see from her shore to the opposite shore—from slavery to freedom!

Then she heard it again. Snarling. Teeth gnashing. Something was definitely in the woods ready to pounce.

She came to a halt, panting loudly, hands shaking with frustration. Her mind searched desperately for an answer. It came to her—chicken thighs.

Although she couldn't make out what it was, she could see the underbrush trembling and felt the echo of the animal's brutal growls.

Eliza edged around, leading the animal away from the shoreline. At the moment, she was staring down a small hill that separated her from the river.

Her fingers deftly maneuvered inside the flour-sack pouch she'd used to stash the little bits of food she'd taken. The baby continued to screech.

Eliza, heart thudding, snatched a chicken thigh from the pouch. As soon as the cooked meat's scent hit the air, Eliza heard the animal growl louder. She caught a glimpse of the beast.

A wolf! she thought. *It's a wolf.*

A second later, when the chicken hit the frozen ground, Eliza heard a frenzy of teeth gnashing at meat and bone. She turned to the river.

Its gleaming expanse, frosted in snow, beckoned her.

Harry's chubby face was contorted as he continued to cry. Eliza realized with agony that her boy was probably just as hungry as the wolf. She felt there was no greater horror than the realization of not being able to protect—or feed—her child.

The wolf quieted, then rustled the bushes. Eliza stood transfixed, realizing he—or she—had finished the meal and come back for more. Her gaze followed the shivering underbrush along the riverbank.

Just as the animal cleared the brush, Eliza leaped toward the river.

In seconds she was on the ice. Ohio was so close, so ready to welcome her and her son. Yet she still had to get there.

Eliza took several steps, gingerly moving across the surface of the ice. She was only several steps away from shore when she heard it. The angry, terrifying sound of the world giving way beneath her feet.

She looked down as cracks were forming. The ice was breaking!

On the shore, the wolf was waiting, walking slowly toward the river. Now it hurled itself onto the ice. Eliza tried to scamper farther onto the river. The animal attempted to lunge, but skidded. The ice beneath it cracked into a large chunk. Unable to keep its balance, the wolf tumbled into the freezing water.

Eliza bit her lip, scared she would soon meet the same fate.

The wolf clawed and clawed against the ice, against the water, moving itself forward until it was back on land. It snarled, shook itself fiercely, then tossed a look of resignation at Eliza before disappearing back into the woods.

Now it was Eliza's turn to make her way back to shore before she drowned. But she weighed more than the animal. Baby Harry must have sensed the terror that gripped his mother. He screamed loudly and tightened his little fists into knots.

The ice shifted beneath her feet. Eliza felt her knees tremble. As she watched, the ice completely broke away from the shore. She and Harry were trapped on an ice floe, a fat chunk of ice that floated on the river. Her skirt dipped into the frigid water. Soon her skin was cold and wet.

She had no idea how she was going to get across the river to Ohio. She couldn't. Not like this.

Turning back to the Kentucky shoreline, Eliza dipped her hand into the freezing water and paddled, steering her way to land. It only took a few moments and she was back—back on land where she was a slave. Her shoulders sagged. Her heart sank. She was hungry and tired, with a baby who was also hungry and tired.

"I will not stop trying, Harry," she vowed again, thinking of so many other women and men who'd tried to escape but failed. So few slaves ever escaped at all. She needed rest so badly that she wanted to cry. In her mind, she could almost smell the hotcakes and sausage that Miss Mattie would sometimes cook for breakfast.

Was she hallucinating?

She could swear she smelled maple syrup!

Eliza slumped over her child, weary, trying to determine her next step. Only her mind wouldn't work. Her arms and legs were wet and cold. Her body had started to shake.

Then a hand lay itself on the back of her shawl. A light touch. Whisper-light. Was she imagining that, too?

A voice spoke, forcing her to turn. She was face-to-face with a large man carrying a shotgun. His serious eyes scowled.

"You better come with me," he said in a gruff whisper.

Not a hallucination, thought Eliza.

He was real!

Chapter Five

REST, RELAX . . . RUN!

Eliza tried to shrink away from the man's touch. Harry whimpered.

"Miz lady," the man said.

"Don't you come near my baby!" she said, her voice quivering. Eliza fell back on her elbow, her son's head tucked against her bosom.

Eliza glared up at the man. He wasn't as old as she'd first thought. He wasn't white, either. Clearly of mixed blood, the man appeared to be a farmer with moss-colored eyes and the bushiest mustache Eliza had ever seen.

He took a step back, then slowly, gently sank to one knee.

“Ma’am, I mean you no harm. I–I heard them wolves, then heard yo’ boy. Came over here ’cause I thought someone needed help.” His voice tapered off, his eyes never leaving her face. Eliza realized his expression was one of fear mixed with admiration. When he reached for her hand, she took his.

“I’m Hiram Johnson,” he said. “Folks all call me Red.”

Eliza ventured a smile as Red helped her to her feet. He was a tall man with boxy hands and skin the palest shade of brown imaginable. And his hair was way more red than brown, telling Eliza everything she needed to know about how he got his nickname.

Red reached out and plucked Harry from the damp sheet-sling easy as pie. He cooed at the boy before looking at Eliza and saying, “Come on, I ’spect you need a meal and some place to sleep.”

A whiff of maple syrup floated off Red, and Eliza realized he smelled like pancakes and sausage. Harry must’ve thought so, too, because he was delighted in the stranger’s arms, no doubt anticipating a feast.

"You escape too?" Eliza asked, once she caught her breath.

"Me and my brother bought our freedom," he said. "We came out of the Deep South. Mississippi."

Eliza exchanged a glance with Red. She'd heard hushed whispers about the brutality and cruelty experienced by slaves in Mississippi, hundreds of miles to the south.

Red shrugged. "Our master was dying, didn't have no close kin. He let us work for our freedom and we was lucky enough to get it settled fo' he died. Come on, I'll let you meet my wife and children."

Following the tall redheaded black man, Eliza found herself and her baby led to a small farmhouse tucked against the edge of the woods. Red explained that he had his own farm, which he worked with his family.

He introduced Eliza to his wife, June, and their three children. They offered her dry clothes and let her lie down to rest. As much as she wanted to help these kind people, once she removed her tattered old shoes and sank onto the mattress,

Eliza found herself being pulled into a sleep as thick and dark as the river.

She wasn't sure how much time had passed when she awoke to find she was covered in multiple blankets, some hand-crocheted. She found herself curled up beside Harry on a straw bed. The covers and hospitality felt like heaven. Surely these kind strangers were angels.

But she knew she was still in danger and couldn't stay here much longer. If her former master and his overseer were out searching, it was only a matter of time before they found the small farm.

She didn't want to be a burden, or to put the family at risk, that was for sure. At breakfast, she helped June. Then she helped the children milk cows and care for the few chickens. All the while her mind churned. How was she going to cross that blasted river if it wasn't frozen solid?

The sun had begun to set on Eliza's first day away from the Seldons. However, as soon as darkness began leaking through the windows, Eliza knew she must go. She stood in the kitchen with

Red and his wife as she considered her next steps.

Then the farmer's youngest boy, his dark eyes wide, burst into the kitchen, yelling, "Mama!" The sound sent ice threading through Eliza's soul.

"What's wrong, child?" the boy's mama asked.

"There's men," he said. "With guns! I was outside, at the edge of the yard, and Jeb came up and told me."

Eliza drew a sharp breath. So did the farmer's wife.

"Who told you men were coming?" Eliza said.

"Jeb did. Jeb Heath. He a white boy whose family is abolitionists. They don't like slavers coming up here causing trouble!" The boy's words spilled in a jumble.

"How far away?" June asked her son, taking him by the shoulders.

"Not far, ma'am. Jeb came on his horse. You know the one? Gunpowder. That's what he calls her—"

"Close by?" Red asked, interrupting the boy. "Did Jeb say they were close by?"

"Yes, sir!" he said. "He told me the men was

looking for a escaped slave lady and her boy!" His words rushed toward Eliza like an overseer's whip, full of pain and menace.

"You didn't tell him nothing, did you?" his mama asked.

"No ma'am!" came his quick reply.

Eliza remembered that there was a small pasture to the rear and west side of the house. To the east lay a thicket of trees separating land from river. While helping with the family chores earlier she'd paid attention to her surroundings, her mind constantly trying to work out the best way to leave.

Now, looking from Red to June, she knew she didn't have a second to spare. Eliza scooped her baby into her arms.

No sooner had she hefted the child against her shoulders than she heard the sound of hoofbeats.

The Seldons' men were coming!

They all understood what it meant—every last one of them in that kitchen. Wordlessly, June tossed a small blanket to Eliza, who grabbed on to it and tucked it around her child. It was the crocheted blanket that had kept Harry and her warm through the night.

June smiled and gave a slight nod of her head. The smile slid away as the three adults turned to the front wall of the house.

The hoofbeats were growing louder.

Shouts rose above the sound of horses beating a path to their door.

Eliza was tired of being afraid. Tired of having a master and being treated like a child. She was a grown woman. A mother. A human being. It was time to make a stand.

The voices grew closer.

Trembling earth rumbled from the ferocity of the horses, then quieted. The horses were slowing down. They were close.

Eliza pushed open the only door to the farmhouse. Through the bare branches of trees that sat up along the road, she saw several men dismounting their horses.

With guns!

She plunged herself headlong into the cold air, with Harry bundled in the blanket, sucking on a carrot. She did not look back.

Eliza lifted the baby to her shoulder.

Then she ran like her life depended on it—a fact that became clear when she heard the crack of a gunshot.

"I see her! There!" someone shouted.

"Don't shoot, you might kill her—and the baby!" came another voice.

Eliza kept running. She couldn't stop now.

Heavy footfalls crashed through brush. Eliza sprinted for the river's edge.

Someone yelled, "Don't get on that ice! You gonna kill yo'self and that baby!"

Still, Eliza kept going.

She had hoped to arrive at night to allow time for the ice to harden. Instead, she had arrived at the end of the day, and the expanse between Kentucky and Ohio was littered with chunks of ice. They floated lazily past. But she could not stop now.

Flinging a desperate prayer at the good Lord above, Eliza held on to Harry tightly and leapt from the shore. Her feet skittered when her thin shoes made contact with the ice. Even so, she didn't fall. Not at first. She crouched, heaving to catch her breath.

"STOP!" came a cry behind her.

She didn't stop. And she didn't look back.

She took another deep breath and jumped over the rushing waters to another large raft of ice. She crouched on hands and knees, with Harry lying on the ice floe. Behind them on the shore, the pursuers barked as loud as their hound dogs, demanding she return.

Eliza twisted around. Lined-up, angry red faces

melted into blackening shadows. It was the posse sent to hunt her down, with Mr. Seldon right in the middle of them all. Six or seven men approached the ice—one of them testing his weight on it.

An anguished sound escaped Eliza's throat. She wanted to growl and gnash her teeth like the wolf from the day before. Instead, she saw a chance to lift Harry onto a larger block of ice ahead. Carefully, she slid the baby to safety, swaddled snugly in the crocheted blanket. Right then, her own cake of ice splintered and Eliza slid into the cold, dark water.

As she dipped below the surface, she heard Harry let out a gusty wail. A thousand warnings about slaves drowning pressed into her soul. It was black as death under the water. Eliza wanted to scream. The water instantly weighed down on her.

Reaching blindly, Eliza clawed at the surface until her hand hit ice again. It was Harry's ice floe. Her fingers slipped and slipped. After several attempts, she managed to get her hands and her forearms over the ice without tipping it.

Harry's face was scrunched up and the air was

alive with his screams. Panting, Eliza clung to the ice, kicking her feet, pushing herself and Harry farther from their pursuers.

The ice-cold water took her breath away. She slogged through the frigid river, not caring one bit about her clothes getting wet. She didn't care how cold she was. All that mattered was keeping Harry safe and never looking back.

Eliza heard the men yelling. Determination burned inside her soul. She did not look back. Instead, she concentrated on the riverbank ahead.

Her teeth chattered. Her fingers were growing numb.

Chunks of river ice floated and butted up against each other. The river was not all that wide, and Eliza could easily see the shore of Ohio ahead.

Shouts behind her continued. Another gunshot pierced the air. Eliza spotted a new slab of ice, bigger and wider. She guided the piece carrying Harry in its direction. Once she was closer to the large slab, she let go of Harry's and, with all the strength she could muster, finally hoisted her entire body back onto the ice. Then she quickly reached over and drew her baby to her side, careful to keep his blanket as dry as possible. His cries turned to murmurs. Numbness danced through her nerve endings and fear of freezing to death set fire to her resolve.

I can't give up.

I can't lose Harry.

I can't let 'em get us.

The phrases repeated in her head. Her icy fingers ached. Still, the Ohio shore appeared closer, and she realized that she and Harry had reached a larger, sturdier-looking island of ice. Moving carefully, she held her baby up and again stepped to the next chunk of ice. Miraculously, rather than being afraid, the baby seemed to delight in this new adventure. He gurgled and clapped his chubby hands.

"Mama!" he exclaimed.

Eliza's lungs felt as though they might explode. Gusts of air rushed in and out of her body. Tears streamed down her cheeks the closer she grew to Ohio.

In the distance, the shouts of her pursuers were growing faint. Energized by the joy on her baby's face, Eliza flung herself onto the next ice floe, her dress heavy and freezing on her legs. Her ragged shoes had all but disintegrated.

When she finally reached the shore, Eliza was exhausted. She lay on the banks catching her breath when suddenly, a man came forward from the shadows. He was a black man who, like the farmer, understood instantly what was happening.

"You came 'cross that river like Jesus walking on water!" he said.

Eliza's legs felt like oatmeal. Yet the fire for freedom burned inside her.

"Can you help me and my boy?" she rasped.

"Come on," he said with a nod. He shook his head. "You soaked through to the bone, but your boy here don't look like he got a drop on him."

Eliza wanted to beam with pride for keeping her son dry and safe. However, all she could do was stumble, no longer able to feel her toes or her feet—or her face.

When she staggered a second time, she almost

dropped her baby. The man caught the boy, who was cooing and laughing and clapping as though all this was just a great adventure.

"I . . ." Her voice came out in a croak. "I—I am Eliza Harris."

Chapter Six

A HUNDRED STEPS TO FREEDOM

The man led Eliza away from the water and into a grouping of trees. She sat and breathed deeply, shivering from the cold ravishing her body. Her heart pounded as though she were still paddling across the river.

She looked at the man and tried to smile. He had narrow shoulders and tired eyes.

"Thank you for helping me," she said. He nodded toward her and patted her hand.

"Can't sit out here for long," he said. "I 'spect folks over yonder might be coming to look for you eventually."

Winded and numb, Eliza gave the barest of

nods. Night was falling fast.

"You need help, don't 'cha?" the man said.

"Yessir, I do," came Eliza's reply. "We both do."

With exhaustion setting in, Eliza could do little more than follow as the man led her away from the river.

"I figure you're tired, but we don't have far to go. I know just the people you need to meet. Think you ready?" he said.

Eliza practically snorted. Darned right she was ready. She wanted to be as far away from Kentucky as possible. She couldn't wait to start her life over.

"You know how to get me up North?" she asked.

"Like I said, I know who can help you, yes I do," he said.

Ready as she was, however, she still felt wobbly. Going in and out of the frozen water and lying atop the ice floes had left her with almost no feeling in her legs and feet. She had heard about frostbite—had seen what it could do. She prayed that after all she'd been through she wouldn't wind up losing a toe—or more.

Casting a glance back toward the water, she knew she didn't have much time. Her pursuers would not stop until they had caught her.

She nodded at the man and said, "Let's get on with it!"

They set out beneath a night sky brilliant with stars. He hoisted Harry in his arms same as Red had done, while Eliza hobbled along trying to regain all the feeling in her legs and feet and hands.

Her guide was silent, except for a question or comment here or there, which he whispered. Eliza understood. Night air carried sound, and sound could get you killed.

They stopped at the bottom of a hill and looked up at the stately house atop of it.

The man pointed. "This is it," he said.

Eliza gazed up at the solid brick manse.

"Who lives here?" Eliza asked. The house seemed both grand and remote, its windows looking down at her.

The man gave a little laugh. "That there's the Rankin House," he said, saying it like everybody

ought to know what that meant. An enormous lump pressed the back of her throat. Eliza did not know what the Rankin House was or why they were there.

The man smiled reassuringly and passed Baby Harry back into Eliza's arms. "You and your young'un go right up this little hill and over that fence. Then climb the steps and let yo'self in," he said.

Eliza's eyes widened. This man must be mad. No way a black woman could just walk into what surely must be a white man's house.

Seeming to sense her hesitation, the kind stranger said, "They will take real good care of you. Feed you and your boy real good."

Eliza's teeth chattered. Harry felt tiny and solid in her arms. She stared up the staircase, remembering tales of such a house, a door to freedom that hovered three hundred feet above the ground. A hundred stone steps led from bottom to top.

Eliza's legs still felt stiff from the cold. Her stomach growled and her son whimpered.

He must be hungry, too, she thought.

"Go on," the man encouraged.

She pulled herself up straight. She hadn't come this far to quit now.

Her knees buckled as she started alone with her baby toward the wood rail fence. Moonlight made the night as glossy as black shoe polish. Her leg muscles cramped and her back ached. The gnawing in her belly began to feel like fire. Tears burned at the corners of her eyes. She wasn't going to give up. No, indeed!

As soon as her feet cleared the fence, Eliza made her way to the stairs. She drew in a deep breath and began to climb.

One step turned to two; then two more. Before long she was halfway up the staircase, trying not to look down. Had she ever been so high up before in her life?

Sweet Mother and Mary, it's like I'm flying!

Step after step, she pushed herself upward, Harry firmly in her arms. Muscles in her legs and backside screamed from the effort, but she did not stop. She was two steps from the top when she shifted her gaze to take in the glittering ice on the river below. Under the night sky, the partially frozen river shimmered like jewels—a bounty from heaven. Eliza felt in her soul that she was in God's hands now. She was where she was supposed to be.

With one final glance, Eliza pushed open the door of the house and went inside.

Eliza found herself in the kitchen. She used a poker to stir logs in a dying fire. A man entered the kitchen. Eliza felt the weight of the firebrand drop from her hand. The iron clattered on the stone floor. Silently, the man retrieved the fallen poker and added more logs to the fire.

He looked at Eliza and said, "I'm John Rankin. This is my house. You're gonna be all right now, Miss. Providence has brought you this far, the good Lord won't abandon you now."

The man excused himself and disappeared into another part of the vast house. Minutes later, a girl, her face pale but pink-cheeked in the firelight, introduced herself as Isabelle, one of the man's daughters.

"Welcome," the girl said.

Before long, despite the late hour, the kitchen was buzzing with activity. Eliza watched in stunned silence as Mr. Rankin's wife, Jean, fussed over Harry while Isabelle handed Eliza dry petticoats and dresses.

Eliza changed and then sat in the kitchen eating a meal. These white folks had accepted her and treated her like a person. Not a slave. The idea wiggled around inside her, almost producing a smile. So this was what freedom was like!

"It's time," said the man called Mr. John Rankin. He had sent his sons out to bring around two horses. Eliza gripped Harry as she and several members of the family made their way back down the hundred steps. Once they were all on level ground, one of Mr. Rankin's sons produced a stepping block so Eliza could climb onto the first horse's back. Then Mrs. Rankin carried forth a red-checked apron wrapped around Eliza's wet clothes, and she hung it on the saddle horn.

Mr. Rankin directed his other son present to accompany Eliza on the next part of her long journey. He told them they would need to go at least seven miles to get to their next destination.

"You will have plenty of time to arrive before daylight. Return when it suits you, for the ice will be flowing and no lawmen will be able to cross that river for several days," Rankin said to his son.

THE RANKIN HOUSE

Reverend John Rankin was born in Tennessee in 1793. His vocal antislavery sermons and sentiments did not sit well with many of his slave-holding neighbors. In 1822, he decided to move to a free state. Ripley, Ohio, was along the Ohio River and possessed a growing community of folks who were willing to help people escaping slavery.

The religious man moved his wife and growing family into a home in the small Ohio riverfront town. In 1825, Rankin built another house in Ripley, high atop a hill. It overlooked the river and was close enough to provide excellent escape routes for slaves and conductors needing safe passage. Legend has it that Rankin's family used to hang a lantern in the window to let slaves and other "conductors" know when it was safe to cross the river.

The Rankin Home was such an active "station" on the Underground Railroad, it is now a National Historic Landmark, honoring the former minister and one of Ohio's most respected abolitionists, who raised thirteen children in the house that served as a safe haven for at least two thousand escaped slaves on their way to freedom. Visitors today can still climb the one hundred steps at the rear of the house, which overlooks the Ohio River.

Just days earlier Eliza could not have imagined anything like this. It felt unreal and a little unsettling. This family, these people who seemed to share so much more with the Seldons than they did with her and the other enslaved people, were risking their safety and the safety of their entire family to help her.

Nothing could erase the memories of all that slavery had taken from her—parents, family, friends. She thought of George, her husband, and wondered if he had made it to Canada. She also wondered if she would ever see him again.

Being out of Kentucky, she knew, was only the first step. There were many more steps in her journey. Eliza drew a deep, shaky breath. Yes, the Rankin House was a place she wouldn't soon forget.

Over the next week, Eliza found herself embarking on one expedition after another. She had heard tales about networks of folks helping slaves escape. Heard the disappearing slaves described as seeming to vanish into hillsides, as if sucked into holes in the earth.

Now she was learning the truth. She and Harry and the people helping—black and white—were not invisible or vanishing. They were simply smart and brave. In the days to come, she passed through Decatur, Cherry Fork, and Washington Court House, through a series of Presbyterian churches, then finally, Cleveland.

Eliza felt near total exhaustion by the time she

and Harry arrived in Cleveland. The Presbyterians here wanted to send her one last step west to deter any slave hunters. After eating and gathering her strength, Eliza was on the move again.

It's all so confusing, Eliza thought days later, as she once again was heading north. She was now at her final stop before crossing into Canada: Detroit, Michigan, where another river—the Detroit—separated her from her ultimate freedom. Escaped slaves were not safe in the North because they could be captured and forced to return. Slave hunters were not permitted to capture or apprehend former slaves in Canada.

Soft snowflakes sifted down around her. Harry romped in the icy fluff, squealing as he played with another little boy, the son of a fellow traveler. Eliza inhaled deeply, the sharp, brittle taste of winter chilling her lungs and making her feel alive. She felt as giddy as the children she was tending. A strange, light feeling touched her skin and her soul.

Hopefulness.

She could picture her husband—a free man.

Picture herself free to finally live with him as a wife should—with their son, too. What so many folks took for granted would soon be a dream come true. Slaves didn't have the right to marry and live together and raise children, unless their master said so.

Eliza thought that it wouldn't be long now before she and George could be together. She would ask everyone she met in Canada until she found him. The thought of how happy and proud he was going to be to see her and Harry made Eliza shiver.

Her life had changed tremendously in a short period of time. The Seldons had fluttered to the outstretches of her memory. Where once they loomed large because of the power they had over her, now she could barely recall the sound of their voices.

"It sure is pretty, ain't it?" asked the mother of the little boy now rolling around in the snow with Harry. The woman also escaping to Canada stood shoulder to shoulder with Eliza. They stared across the narrow expanse that separated Michigan from their future.

“Sure is,” Eliza said. “It sure is!”

That evening it was time to go. The sun shrank beneath the horizon. Thorny pines and bare elms etched inky silhouettes against the diminishing daylight.

Eliza, Harry, and the other black woman and child were led to a church on the northern edge of town. Second Baptist Church had begun helping escaped slaves cross into Canada. Harry clung to Eliza’s arm as they made their way down the narrow passage into the basement.

Eliza and a few other passengers were led out of the church’s basement, down a narrow path to the river’s edge, and onto boats. It was a cold night, but without much wind. The dark water was flat as the silver moon, which lay winking at the group like a coin in black velvet.

She became aware of shapes and sounds and smells. A thousand trees standing together, branches and leaves intertwined; the slurping of the river against the side of the boat; and the briny scent of the night air.

America.

Would this be the last time she ever laid eyes on the nation she once called home?

With another look over her shoulder, Eliza couldn't help wondering about all the souls she was leaving behind. Miss Maddie and Sadie. The other mothers and sons, sisters and brothers, all those who'd remain enslaved.

She pulled Harry against her, shushing his voice for one last time. It wouldn't be long before her boy would be able to make noise and sing, play, laugh, or cry loud as he wanted to. No need to worry that his cries would draw unwanted attention that could lead to a slaver's lash.

The boat drifted northward, rocking gently, steadily, the North Star still guiding her.

By morning, she would truly be free.

AUTHOR'S NOTE

WHAT I LEARNED ABOUT THE REAL ELIZA HARRIS!

Before embarking on this project, I knew nothing about Eliza Harris. I was not familiar with the tale of an African American slave woman's desperate escape from a Kentucky plantation, crossing the frozen Ohio River with her baby. After doing weeks of research, making phone calls, and downloading digital copies of antique books, what I know about the enigmatic woman whose daring escape made her an icon of slavery and the Underground Railroad has, quite frankly, blown my mind.

Eliza Harris as the world came to know her was a composite—a mixture of people lumped together by author Harriet Beecher Stowe to create a secondary character for her nineteenth-century novel *Uncle Tom's Cabin*. Don't get me wrong, by all accounts there was an Eliza (last name unknown).

In 1838 or 1839 a real slave woman called Eliza

escaped her Kentucky plantation. While slave catchers dogged her heels and the vision of a free state across the Ohio River drove her forward, the woman dashed into the frozen waters and fought her way to freedom. Some accounts include her baby son; some do not.

What blows my mind, however, is that Stowe learned about Eliza's escape during a trip to Kentucky—heard the story, but never met the woman. Stowe, an ardent abolitionist who felt pushed beyond her limits with the passing of the Fugitive Slave Act of 1850 (see Fugitive Slave Laws sidebar), decided to write something for an abolitionist newspaper to stoke America's passion for freeing slaves. So she included a character in her book based on the story of the woman who risked drowning rather than remain a slave.

Well, here's the mind-blowing part. Stowe's novel gained so much popularity that a few years later she felt compelled to write a new book, *A Key to Uncle Tom's Cabin*, to answer proslavery critics who claimed she was sensationalizing the treatment of slaves. She outlined in her research how she based characters and events in *Uncle Tom's Cabin* on real-life people and incidents. In the section on Eliza Harris, she admits that the description of Eliza in her runaway best seller was based on a mixed-race woman she'd spotted in church in Kentucky years after the real Eliza had made her escape. Yet, for a hundred years or more, Stowe's idealized version of Eliza—from her "silky black hair" to her "finely moulded shape"—remained the portrait that fueled artwork, stage plays, books, and later movies.

I was fascinated to read in Keith Griffler's essay "Beyond the Quest for the 'Real Eliza Harris': Fugitive Slave Women in the Ohio Valley" that Eliza was actually believed to be in her early forties, stoutly built, and anything but a delicate woman. History has always intrigued me, and the history surrounding Stowe, *Uncle Tom's Cabin*, and the character and real woman Eliza Harris shows us how perceptions can become reality and reality can bend toward perception. Separating fact from fiction is hard since most of what we know of her real life is based on the fictionalized version described by Stowe.

Readers, here's what you need to know: There was a woman who was desperate to escape life as a slave, and upon learning that her master wanted to sell her child, she reacted by snatching up the baby and crossing the frozen river. Despite the river breaking into chunks beneath her and the baby, she continued to fight and claw until she reached the other side. Once she arrived, she was taken into the home of one of America's well-known abolitionists, John Rankin, in Ripley, Ohio, who arranged for her a journey in which she was ferried from one Underground Railroad station to another, ultimately finding true freedom in Canada, where no slave hunter could follow. I dramatized parts of the tale of her escape simply because no one knows the intimate details of her journey. Eliza couldn't read or write; she didn't leave letters or notes that described her inner feelings. If she could've taken selfies in the Kentucky woods and beyond, it would have been fabulous. However, no such documentation exists. I've done my best to concentrate on how one might feel during these events. Was the real Eliza threatened by wolves or coyotes? Who knows? But she was on the run in the dark in the woods in winter, where there were not a lot of food sources for these nighttime hunters. I hope you enjoy this version of the escape of Eliza Harris.

HARRIET BEECHER STOWE (JUNE 14, 1811–JULY 1, 1896)

"Is this the little woman who wrote the book that made the great war?"

—attributed to President Abraham Lincoln, on the day he met Stowe

Words have power. When Lincoln met with author Harriet Beecher Stowe on December 2, 1862, he almost certainly was acknowledging that her words helped to push a nation to fight against an ugly institution.

Many years before, in 1851, Stowe, who was already a prolific writer, felt compelled to share her views on the institution of slavery. She approached the publisher of an antislavery newspaper to ask if she could "paint a word picture of slavery." *The National Era* agreed, and Stowe set forth to write a three- or four-part series. The public craved more. She ultimately wrote forty parts to her "word picture" and created a national stir. In 1852, her newspaper series became a two-part book—*Uncle Tom's Cabin.*

An article in the *New York Independent* published May 20, 1852, states: "A SALE unprecedented in the history of book-selling in America. On the 20th of March the first sale was made of the unparalleled book, and in sixty days 50,000 copies, making 100,000 Volumes have been sold." Over three hundred thousand copies were sold in the United States in the book's first year, while 1.5 million copies were sold in Great Britain.

Did the popularity of her book ultimately lead to the Civil War? Probably not by itself, but its prominence during the time period added huge weight to the argument against slavery.

THE IMMORTALITY OF ELIZA

So much about the enduring nature of Eliza Harris's popularity hovers between legend and fact. An unknown slave woman escaped from her Kentucky plantation in the winter of 1838 to prevent her master from selling her two-year-old son to another plantation. Author Harriet Beecher Stowe, upon learning of the nameless woman's courage and determination to cross a not-quite-frozen river and risk death rather than lose her child, heard the story and gave the woman a name—Eliza Harris.

Eliza Harris's character appears in *Uncle Tom's Cabin* as a short, dramatic subplot, depicting a caramel-complexioned, biracial woman and her cherubic baby.

Uncle Tom's Cabin became such a massive hit in the 1800s that shortly thereafter it spawned an entire entertainment cottage industry. A huge part of that popularity was owed to the nation's—and the world's—reaction to the plight of a practically invisible slave woman's journey.

In Patricia A. Turner's essay, "The Rise and Fall of Eliza Harris," she states, "In the nineteenth century, the novel was so popular that it triggered numerous stage productions, making Stowe's story the most commonly produced theatrical program from the mid-1850s until at least the beginning of the twentieth century. Theatrical versions of *Uncle Tom's Cabin* were so popular they spawned their own vocabulary. They were called Tom Shows, and the actors and actresses who performed in them were called Tommers."

Scriptwriters often reorganized Stowe's novel, giving Eliza and her fate a larger role. Along with the stage shows, Eliza was also the subject of many art renderings, posters, engravings, and paintings. Her character even played a major part in a 1903 silent movie called *Uncle Tom's Cabin*.

Stowe wrote that she created the image of Eliza based on an entirely different woman she spotted one day in a Kentucky church. The real Eliza was almost certainly stout and dark-skinned. Even so, artists of all leanings pictured Eliza as near a white woman as possible. The more time passed, the less the image of Eliza Harris resembled a person of African descent.

A beautifully rendered version by famous artist Adolphe Jean-Baptiste Bayot has a sort of passion and urgency often found in biblical artwork. Subtle blushes of pink sky and pink skin contrast with inky grays and blacks used to promote a feeling of cold and despair. If you didn't know the woman and child were escaping slavery, surely the color of their skin would give no clue.

Fact may be stranger than fiction, but sometimes fiction looms larger than fact. The woman known as Eliza became an icon based on a rumor.

FUGITIVE SLAVE LAWS

The preamble to the US Constitution states:

We the People of the United States, in Order to form a more perfect Union, establish Justice, ensure domestic Tranquility, provide for the common defence, promote the general Welfare, and secure the Blessings of Liberty to ourselves and our Posterity, do ordain and establish this Constitution for the United States of America.

A great and powerful sentence. However, it is the meaning of the first three words, "We the People," as interpreted differently by different people, that would lead to centuries of dissension. Because "People," as interpreted by the adult white males who ran American society at the time, did not refer to women, Native Americans, or African Americans. Slaves were not considered whole people; they were property.

The Fugitive Slave Act of 1793 empowered slave

owners to travel into other states and territories to reclaim their "property" if a slave escaped. However, it didn't compel people of those states to assist. While it was unlawful and punishable by a $500 fine for someone to knowingly hide, conceal, or withhold a slave, the act did not prohibit a citizen from providing assistance to someone who might or might not be an escaped slave.

The second law, the Fugitive Slave Act of 1850, required marshals and lawmen in other states to assist in the capture and return of escaped slaves regardless of the laws of their states.

Think about this: between 1525 and 1860, twelve million Africans were snatched from their homes and brought to the New World for slavery, according to Henry Louis Gates, Jr. in a 2014 article in The Root. By 1850, slave labor had grown increasingly important. Of the 3.2 million slaves working in fifteen slave states in 1850, 1.8 million worked on cotton fields. And the cost of purchasing a slave had risen from "$500 in New Orleans in 1800, to $1,800 by 1860." That was a lot of money back then. Plantation owners were desperate to hold onto their investments—even if their investments were humans forced to live and work in harsh conditions.

Interestingly enough, it was the enactment of the 1850 law—and her personal experience meeting and hearing the stories of escaped slaves—that spurred Harriet Beecher Stowe to write the short stories that would later become *Uncle Tom's Cabin.*

IMPORTANT ABOLITIONISTS

Not all Americans supported the practice of slavery. In fact, the Civil War (1861–1865) was fought because President Lincoln wanted to stop the spread of slavery and southern states wanted to preserve the practice. Abolitionists were activists—young and old, black and white—who wanted to end slavery. They offered aid to escaped slaves in a variety of ways: by providing clothing, food, and transportation for escapees traveling north. They risked their lives by opening their homes to shelter them.

And they wrote articles, published newspapers, and traveled around the country lecturing about the need to abolish slavery for good.

African Americans who lived in the North were free, even though racial prejudice impacted their lives, too. Still, they were able to work, marry, read, and otherwise function like other human beings. Slaves had no such freedom. Abolitionists wanted to help slaves find freedom and transition into their new lives. Here are some of the abolitionists who became famous for their contributions and sacrifice:

Harriet Tubman (c. 1822–1913)—Born a slave in Maryland, Tubman escaped in 1849 with two of her brothers. She would return to the South again and again, helping over three hundred slaves find freedom on the Underground Railroad. In addition to helping ferry slaves to freedom, Harriet also served as a spy for the Union during the Civil War, taking secrets across enemy lines to embedded troops. Her role in American history may someday be commemorated by the US Treasury placing her image on the twenty-dollar bill. In 2016, during the Obama administration, the new twenty dollar bill was announced. However, in 2018, during the Trump administration, the redesign was deprioritized. A spokesperson said it could be ten years or more before a redesign is made public.

William Lloyd Garrison (1805–1879)—A newspaper writer and editor who wrote about and supported the abolition movement, Garrison called on his fellow citizens to abolish slavery immediately and for black people to be treated equally in every way. To further the cause of emancipation, Garrison started an abolitionist paper, *The Liberator*, in 1830, which ran weekly for thirty-five years without missing a single issue. When the Civil War ended, he at last saw the abolition of slavery.

Frederick Douglass (1818–1895)—Born Frederick Augustus Washington Bailey in Maryland, Douglass changed his name after escaping slavery and moving to New York. His mother had been a slave who died when Douglass was ten; he never knew his father, who was white and possibly his mother's master. Douglass's upbringing was brutal, filled with unspeakable degradation at the hands of a well-known "slave breaker"—an individual who took pleasure in breaking the "mind, body, and spirit" of a slave to the point that they would not resist. However, the cruelty had the opposite effect on Frederick Douglass. In 1836, he vowed to escape his captivity, but was jailed when his plans were discovered. Two years later, while working for a Baltimore shipyard, Douglass once again set a plan in motion. This time he did not fail. He escaped to New York and ultimately created a home in New Bedford, Massachusetts, with his new bride whom he'd married in New York City. It was here that Douglass began his life's work—illuminating hearts and minds to the hardships and indignities of slavery. He saw William Lloyd Garrison speak in Bristol at the Anti-Slavery Society's annual meeting. Douglass was so moved by the speaker that he said, "No face and form ever impressed me with such sentiments [the hatred of slavery] as did those of William Lloyd Garrison."

After being invited to become a speaker for the

Anti-Slavery Society, Douglass set aside fear of reprisal for his escape and published *Narrative of the Life of Frederick Douglass, An American Slave, Written by Himself,* in 1845. The former-slave-turned-author toured Europe speaking about the book, his life, and the institution of slavery, establishing himself as an abolitionist with first-hand knowledge.

John Rankin (1793–1886)—A Presbyterian minister most of his life, Rankin opened his home to escaped slaves and was a conductor on the Underground Railroad. He tried starting an antislavery organization in Kentucky, but was ridiculed for his efforts. Slavery was legal in Kentucky. He moved across the river to Ripley, Ohio, and before long moved into a house on a three-hundred-foot-high hill that overlooked the Ohio River. He provided food and shelter to as many as two thousand escaped slaves while in Ripley, earning himself legend status and a spot in Harriet Beecher Stowe's *Uncle Tom's Cabin.* Many historians believe it was the Rankin family, either John or his son, who first told Harriet Beecher Stowe of an escaped slave woman so determined to cross the river that even after the ice gave way beneath her, the woman continued to fight, lifting her child above her head to cross to freedom—the original Eliza Harris.

Upon learning that his brother Thomas had purchased a slave, John Rankin wrote him a series of letters denouncing slavery that were eventually published as *Letters on American Slavery*. This became the most important publication read by abolitionists at the time.

Levi Coffin (1798–1877)—An abolitionist and conductor on the Underground Railroad, by age fifteen Coffin was helping his family lend aid to slaves escaping from North Carolina farms and plantations. In 1821 he attempted to open a school to help slaves learn to read. It failed, however, because slave owners did not want their slaves to read. A few years later, in 1826, Coffin moved to Indiana, where he would spend the next two decades helping African Americans escape bondage and find freedom. At some point his home became known as Grand Central Station because he conducted so many passengers along the Underground Railroad. After moving to Cincinnati, Ohio, in 1847, Coffin operated the Western Free Produce Association—a store that sold only goods made from free labor. Coffin continued to fight for the freedom of African Americans, and after the Civil War he retired and wrote his memoirs.

AFRICAN AMERICAN WOMEN IN THE ABOLITIONIST MOVEMENT

Harriet Tubman may have been one of the most famous black women associated with the Underground Railroad, but she was by no means the only one. Black women played a major role in the abolitionist movement.

Frances Ellen Watkins Harper (1825–1911)—Author of a poem titled "Eliza Harris" published in 1853 and inspired by Harriet Beecher Stowe's *Uncle Tom's Cabin*, Watkins was a notable orator, author, and abolitionist. She grew up with her maternal aunt and uncle after her mother died when she was three. While working as a domestic in a Quaker household, Harper had access to literature that likely helped her develop as a writer and speaker. She married in 1860 and in 1892 published her first novel, *Iola Leroy.* She continued to support women and African American causes throughout her life, even cofounding the National Association of Colored Women with Harriet Tubman, as well as many others dedicated to the improvement of life for African American women and families.

Maria W. Stewart (1803–1879)—The first woman in American history to make a speech in public, she demanded to be heard on the subject of human rights and criticized black men for not being more vocal.

Sarah Mapps Douglass (1806–1882)—The freeborn daughter of Robert and Grace Douglass, distinguished members of Philadelphia society, Douglass and her mother founded the Philadelphia Female Anti-Slavery Society in 1833.

The Forten Women—Three generations of Forten women forged lasting contributions to the antislavery cause in the nineteenth century: mother Charlotte; daughters Sarah, Margaretta, and Harriet; and granddaughter Charlotte. The Fortens were huge financial contributors to abolitionist causes, also holding petition drives, publishing pamphlets, and fund-raising.

Harriet Ann Jacobs (1813–1897)—Born a slave in Edenton, North Carolina, Jacobs wanted to escape her master so badly that she finally ran away and hid in her grandmother's cramped attic crawlspace for seven years. She wanted to stay close enough to keep an eye on her two small children, yet safe from the attention of the man who owned her. In 1842, after one of her daughter's had been freed and moved North, Harriet, still considered a fugitive, took action. Disguising herself, she set sail to Philadelphia and then to New York. She would become a nurse and later, an author. She published articles and spoke to audiences in order to advocate and raise funds for recently freed but poverty-stricken former slaves and children orphaned during the Civil War. In *Incidents in the Life of a Slave Girl*, Jacobs describes her harrowing journey to escape the bondage of slavery.

SELECTED BIBLIOGRAPHY

Coffin, Levi. "The Story of Eliza Harris." In *Reminiscences of Levi Coffin, The Reputed President of the Underground Railroad*, 147–150. Cincinnati: Western Tract Society, 1876.

"Find 'Uncle Tom's' Grave in Ontario Town." *The Province Sun*. 1930. August 17, 1930.

"Francis Ellen Watkins Harper." Poetryfoundation.org. https://www.poetryfoundation.org/poets/frances-ellen-watkins-harper.

"Frederick Douglass." PBS.org Resource Bank. http://www.pbs.org/wgbh/aia/part4/4p1539.html.

Griffler, Keith. "Beyond the Quest for the 'Real Eliza Harris': Fugitive Slave Women in the Ohio Valley." *Ohio Valley History* 3, no. 2 (2003): 3–16. https://muse.jhu.edu/article/572714/pdf.

"Levi Coffin." National Park Service. Updated September 14, 2017. https://www.nps.gov/people/levi-coffin.htm.

"Levi Coffin." Ohio History Central. Accessed December 9, 2018. http://www.ohiohistorycentral.org/w/Levi_Coffin.

Jacobs, Harriet. *Incidents in the Life of a Slave Girl*. Penguin Classics, 2000.

"Old Uncle Tom." *The Oskaloosa Independent*. 1878. September 7, 1878.

Rankin, John and Rankin, John, Jr. Rankin family papers. 1830s. Ohio History Connection, collection catalog number VFM 2137, folders 2, 3, 4, and 5.

Stowe, Harriet Beecher. *A Key to Uncle Tom's Cabin*. Boston: John P. Jewett and Company, 1854.

Stowe, Harriet Beecher. *Uncle Tom's Cabin*. Cambridge, MA: Houghton, Mifflin and Company, The Riverside Press, 1895.

"The Rankin House." http://www.ripleyohio.net/htm/rankin.htm.

Turner, Patricia A. "The Rise and Fall of Eliza Harris: From Novel to Tom Shows to Quilts." *Uncle Tom's Cabin and American Culture: A Multi-Media Archive*. University of Virginia. Published 2007. http://utc.iath.virginia.edu/interpret/exhibits/turner/turner.html.

"Uncle Tom 'o Grave." *The Leader Post*. 1930. July 9, 1930.

ABOUT THE AUTHOR

SHERRI WINSTON spent most of her childhood making up stories and reading books. She is proud to be an author for young readers. Her novel *President of the Whole Fifth Grade* was a Sunshine State Young Readers Award selection and *President of the Whole Sixth Grade* received a starred review from *Kirkus Reviews*. Winston is also the author of *The Kayla Chronicles*. Prior to writing fiction, she was a newspaper journalist for many years. Winston is a Michigan native who can't believe she gets to live in Orlando, Florida, and write all day in her bunny slippers. She is mother to two daughters and one bossy lady pup. In addition, she is an avid baker of cupcakes and loves football and photography. To learn more about Winston, go to www.voteforcupcakes.com or www.sherriwinston.wordpress.com.

ABOUT THE EDITOR

MICHAEL TEITELBAUM has been a writer and editor of children's books for more than twenty-five years. He worked on staff as an editor at Golden Books, Grossett & Dunlap, and Macmillan. As a writer, Michael's fiction work includes *The Scary States of America*, fifty short stories—one from each state—all about the paranormal, published by Random House, and *The Very Hungry Zombie: A Parody*, done with artist extraordinaire Jon Apple, published by Skyhorse. His nonfiction work includes *Jackie Robinson: Champion for Equality*, published by Sterling; *The Baseball Hall of Fame*, a two-volume encyclopedia, published by Grolier; *Sports in America, 1980-89*, published by Chelsea House; *Great Moments in Women's Sports*; and *Great Inventions: Radio and Television*, both published by World Almanac Library. Michael lives with his wife, Sheleigah, and two talkative cats in the beautiful Catskill Mountains of upstate New York.

Turn the page for a sneak peek at the next thrilling adventure in the

GREAT ESCAPES SERIES!

Chapter One

THE NEW ARRIVAL

"Yankees, keep it moving!"

On a sweltering-hot September afternoon in 1863, Union colonel Thomas Rose swatted away mosquitoes as he shuffled down the dusty Richmond, Virginia, street. He was one in a long, slow-moving line of captured Union soldiers. Dehydrated and exhausted, the soldiers struggled to keep upright as Confederate guards on horseback barked orders. Yet despite his parched throat and sore, bleeding feet, Rose managed to hold his head high and keep pace with his horse-riding enemy. He refused to let the Confederates, or "Rebels," as he thought of them, see him suffer. Ahead of him in line, a younger officer stumbled and nearly collapsed.

If we don't get some water soon, Rose thought, his black hair and beard dripping with sweat, *we're all gonna keel over . . .*

Rose didn't know where the Confederates were taking the seventy Union soldiers they'd captured. He and his fellow Northerners had come all the way from Chickamauga, Georgia, where they'd been taken prisoner by the Confederates and herded into overcrowded cattle cars. It had taken two days to reach Richmond by train, making stops along the way in South and North Carolina, where they were insulted and spat on by the local townsfolk. The men were given some water but no food, and there was no room to sit or lie down.

Now as Rose marched in the suffocating Virginia heat, his belly ached from hunger.

"Halt!" a Confederate yelled. The prisoners stopped in their tracks.

Rose raised his eyes to peer through a steamy haze of kicked-up dust. Ahead of him, an enormous three-story brick building loomed—Libby Prison.

It looks more like a warehouse than a prison, Rose thought.

Built on the outskirts of town, a few yards from the James River, the monstrous edifice with barred windows was to be his home for the foreseeable future. He realized that if it were this hot outside, inside wouldn't be any cooler. Rose shuddered, knowing that once they entered the prison, some of his fellow soldiers—and even Rose himself—might never leave.

Thunderheads rumbled in the distance, the dark clouds rolling across the sky like advancing cavalry.

As Rose watched, two Confederate officers rode their horses over from the prison stables.

Surely that man riding in front isn't in charge of the prison, Rose thought. *He doesn't look a day over twenty-five.*

"Welcome home, boys," the young man shouted in a thick southern accent from atop his horse. He was sharply dressed in a gray Confederate frock coat, its polished gold buttons almost blinding in the sun. A commanding officer's hat shaded a narrow, clean-shaven face. To Rose, he almost seemed like a kid playing dress-up in his father's clothes. "My name is Major Thomas Turner. I'm the commander of this prison. My second-in-command is the old boy to my right, warden Dick Turner—no relation."

Rose glanced over at the commander's underling. Unlike his boyish-looking superior officer, the older Warden Turner had a scarred face and a yellow, rotten-toothed grin. He held a bullwhip in his right hand.

"Y'all mind the rules, won't no harm come to ya," Major Turner continued. "Step outa line, you'll wish you was dead. See, ol' Dick here used to run a plantation, so he knows how to run a tight ship."

All around Rose, the other prisoners shuffled uneasily. He knew they were thinking of the reports they had heard of the brutal conditions of Southern slave plantations, and the cruel nature of plantation overseers. Rose believed that slavery must be abolished. He was proud to lay his life on the line in honor of that belief. He wasn't alone: if the newspapers were to be believed, more than two million Northerners of all backgrounds were fighting to end slavery and keep the country together. At the same time, about a million Confederates were fighting to hold on to their states' rights to continue the slave trade.

BLACK AMERICANS IN THE CIVIL WAR

Americans of all backgrounds and ethnicities fought in the Civil War. Although exact numbers are unknown, at least 180,000 free black men fought for the Union Army. Some had formerly been enslaved, and some volunteered from as far away as Canada and the Caribbean. By the end of the war, 40,000 black soldiers had given their lives fighting for their right to be free.

Rose watched as Turner, in his gray Confederate uniform, kicked a prisoner who was muttering under his breath. The prisoner fell to the ground.

"No talking!" Turner screamed.

While some others helped the prisoner back to his feet, Turner continued.

"Chow time is twice a day. My rules are simple: keep in line, do your time, and you live. Step out of line or try to escape—you die." He paused and smiled. "Now y'all enjoy your stay."

He nodded to one of the guards, who bellowed, "Inside, now!"

The prisoners began shuffling toward two massive wooden doors. Rose peered up at the towering building. Through the barred windows, he could see the ghostly shadows of the inmates moving around inside.

After he and his fellow prisoners were herded through the doors, a wave of damp heat and rancid air hit Rose like a punch in the face. The young officer who'd nearly collapsed during the march finally toppled over the moment he stepped foot in the building. He lay in a crumpled, convulsing heap on the wood-planked floor. Rose winced as the man began vomiting.

"Get that lazy Yank to his feet," the guard barked.

Rose gritted his teeth and helped peel the

young officer off the floor.

"Stick these boys on the second floor in the lower Chickamauga Room," one of the guards told another, nodding toward a group of prisoners that included Rose. "And put the rest on the third floor. And somebody get this boy off the floor—Lord almighty, what a mess . . ."

Rose followed his fellow prisoners up the creaking wooden staircase. Emerging on the second floor, he grimaced at the sight of the Libby inmates already there. Many were rail-thin and looked as if a strong breeze could knock them over. Yankee uniforms hung loosely from their skeletal frames. Their beards and hair were wild and unkempt but did little to hide gaunt cheeks and sunken eyes. The air was stifling, the stink of a hundred or more unwashed men packed into one room almost unbearable.

How can a man last in this place? Rose thought.

Rose made his way into the room. He saw no cots or blankets for cold nights. Here the prisoners had almost nothing, just a couple of crates and makeshift benches cobbled together from spare wood.

"Welcome to the Chickamauga Room," one of the guards drawled. "Figured it'd be the most appropriate place to stick you boys since that's where y'all were captured."

"I feel at home already," Rose replied without missing a beat.

The guard laughed in return and left the new prisoners to get acquainted with their surroundings.

As Rose looked around, a crack of thunder shook the walls, followed by a collective groan in the room. Some of the men scrambled to their feet, seeming panicked, while the new inmates looked on, confused.

Rain began to pour. As Rose watched the deluge outside the four small, barred windows, he realized he couldn't ignore his scratchy, bone-dry throat a second longer.

"Pardon me, sir, where might I get some water?" he asked a prisoner standing next to him. The man was wearing a major's uniform.

"In that washroom just yonder," the major said. He took his measure of Rose, then handed the colonel a metal cup.

Rose thanked him and headed over to the small room. There was a sink and trough with a legion of flies buzzing around it. The colonel turned the faucet and filled the cup with brackish river water. He had barely wetted his gullet and stuck the cup back under the spigot for a refill when he heard a commotion coming from the first floor.

What's going on down there? he thought, glancing at the stairwell.

Then he felt something crawling on his arm. Looking back, he saw a giant rat on his sleeve.

"AAH!"

Rose screamed and ran out of the room, with the soaked, screeching rat clinging to his uniform. Before the creature could take a bite out of his neck, Rose reached up, grabbed hold of the squirming animal, and threw it to the ground. He watched in disgust as it scurried away. As he looked back into the washroom, to his horror he saw hundreds of rats climbing out of the drain in the trough and through holes in the wall. They emerged from every opening—the windows, the stairwell, and each hole, crack, and cranny in the walls and floorboards.

One older, particularly crazed-looking prisoner with a white beard laughed.

"Say hello to the welcome wagon, fellas!" he cackled.

Rose grimaced, watching in awe as the prisoners knocked the seemingly fearless rodents off their trouser legs in an almost comical dance.

Looking around, he spied the major who had given him the cup calmly observing the scene from his corner. Approaching him, Rose handed the cup back and asked, "What is going on here?"

The major grinned and shook his head. "I should've warned you about the rats. Happens every time it rains. They climb up through the walls to escape the flooding river water. Better get used to it, 'cause it rains quite a bit."

Kicking what had to have been a three-pound rat off his boot, Rose turned to the window and stared out at the river and beyond. *This is no prison*, he thought. *It's the seventh circle of hell. And I'll be damned if I'm going to rot in here!*

Ready For More Risks?
Read the GREAT ESCAPES series!